INDIAN TRAILS
PUBLIC LIBRARY DISTRICT
WHEELING, ILLINOIS 60090
847-459-4100
www.indiantrailslibrary.org

DEMCO

TREASURE ISLAND

Vol. 3: Mutiny on the Hispaniola

Adapted from the novel by ROBERT LOUIS STEVENSON.

THE STORY SO FAR:

*Jim Hawkins relates his adventures as a boy during the quest for Treasure Island: When a rough seaman called **Billy Bones** died of a stroke at his family's "Admiral Benbow" inn on the English coast, Jim and his mother found money and papers... and learned that Billy was once in the crew of the late dreaded pirate **Captain Flint**. Others of that murderous bunch attacked the inn, searching for the map of Treasure Island they knew Billy had possessed. After they fled, Jim enlisted the help of **Dr. Livesey** and **Squire Trelawney** to find the buried treasure.*

*The Squire acquired a schooner, the Hispaniola, and they sailed from Bristol, with **Captain Smollett** in command. Unfortunately, Trelawney had been tricked into hiring the one-legged **Long John Silver** as ship's cook—and Silver, once quartermaster for Flint, secretly hired many of Flint's old crew for the voyage. By luck, Jim overheard Silver and several of the pirates talking about their plans of mutiny, and informed his friends—just as the Hispaniola reached Treasure Island...!*

Writer	Penciler	Inker	Colorist
Roy Thomas	Mario Gully	Pat Davidson	SotoColor's
			A. Crossley

Letterer	Cover	Production
Virtual Calligraphy's	Greg Hildebrandt	Anthony Dial
Joe Caramagna		

Associate Editor	Editor	Editor in Chief	Publisher
Nicole Boose	Ralph Macchio	Joe Quesada	Dan Buckley

VISIT US AT
www.abdopublishing.com

Reinforced library bound edition published in 2009 by Spotlight, a division of the ABDO Group, 8000 West 78th Street, Edina, Minnesota 55439. Spotlight produces high-quality reinforced library bound editions for schools and libraries. Published by agreement with Marvel Characters, Inc.

Library of Congress Cataloging-in-Publication Data

Thomas, Roy, 1940-
  Treasure Island / adapted from the novel by Robert Louis Stevenson ; Roy Thomas, writer ; Mario Gully, penciler ; Pat Davidson, inker ; SotoColor's A. Crossley, colorist ; VC's Joe Caramagna, letterer. -- Reinforced library bound ed.
       v. cm.
  "Marvel."
  Contents: v. 1. Treasure Island -- v. 2. Treasure Island part 2 -- v. 3. Mutiny on the Hispaniola -- v. 4. Embassy--and attack -- v. 5. In the enemy's camp -- v. 6. Pirates' end?
  ISBN 9781599616018 (v. 1) -- ISBN 9781599616025 (v. 2) -- ISBN 9781599616032 (v. 3) -- ISBN 9781599616049 (v. 4) -- ISBN 9781599616056 (v. 5) -- ISBN 9781599616063 (v. 6)
  Summary: Retells, in comic book format, Robert Louis Stevenson's tale of an innkeeper's son who finds a treasure map that leads him to a pirate's fortune.
  [1. Stevenson, Robert Louis, 1850-1894. --Adaptations. 2. Graphic novels. 3. Buried treasure--Fiction. 4.Pirates--Fiction. 5. Adventure and adventurers--Fiction. 6. Caribbean Area--History--18th century--Fiction.] I. Stevenson, Robert Louis, 1850-1894. II. Gully, Mario. III. Davidson, Pat, 1965- IV. Crossley, Andrew.
V. Caramagna, Joe. VI. Title.
PZ7.7.T518 Tre 2009
[Fic]--dc22   2008035322

All Spotlight books have reinforced library bindings and are manufactured in the United States of America.

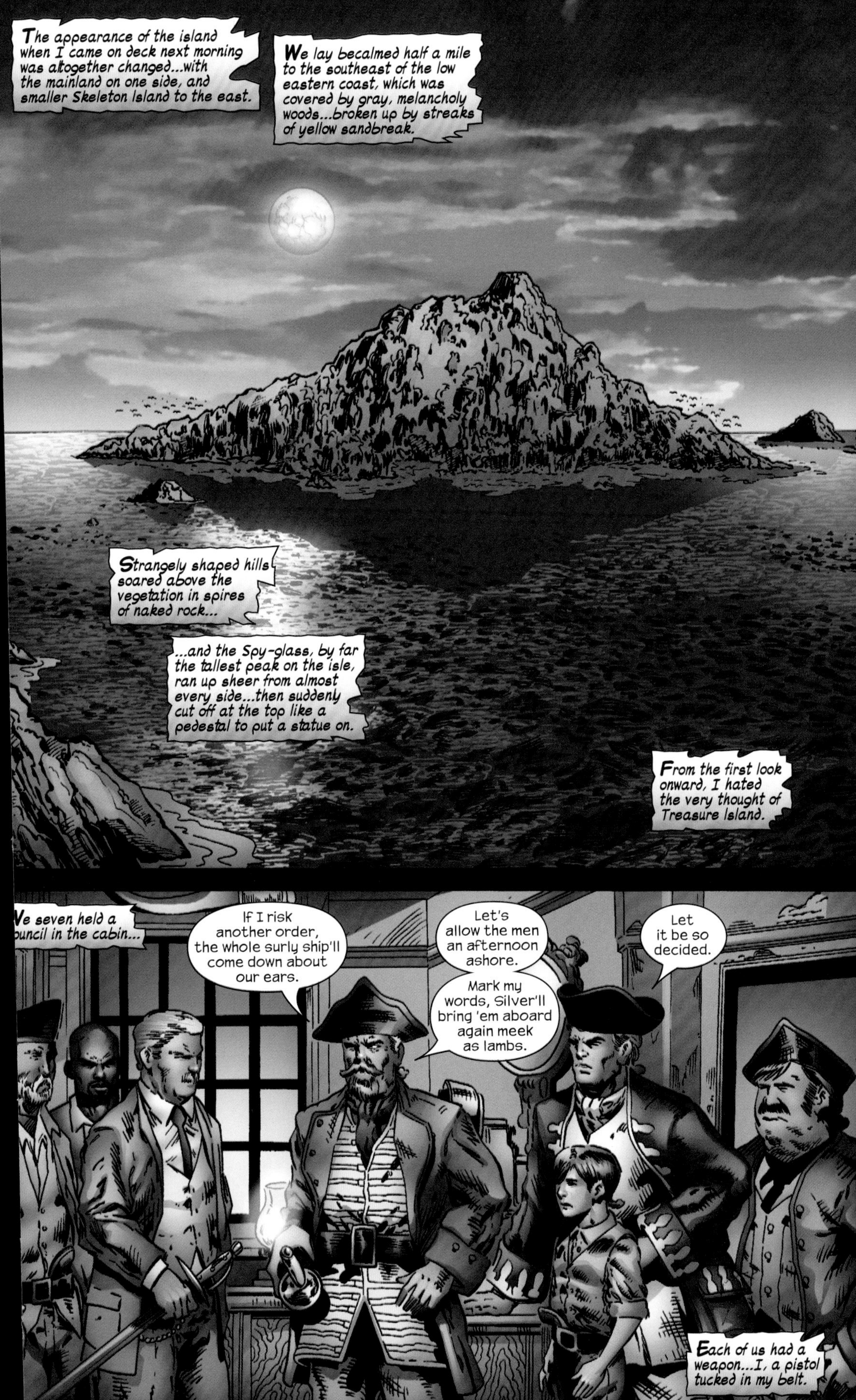
The appearance of the island when I came on deck next morning was altogether changed...with the mainland on one side, and smaller Skeleton Island to the east.
We lay becalmed half a mile to the southeast of the low eastern coast, which was covered by gray, melancholy woods...broken up by streaks of yellow sandbreak.
Strangely shaped hills soared above the vegetation in spires of naked rock...
...and the Spy-glass, by far the tallest peak on the isle, ran up sheer from almost every side...then suddenly cut off at the top like a pedestal to put a statue on.
From the first look onward, I hated the very thought of Treasure Island.
Ve seven held a ouncil in the cabin...
If I risk another order, the whole surly ship'll come down about our ears.
Let's allow the men an afternoon ashore.
Mark my words, Silver'll bring 'em aboard again meek as lambs.
Let it be so decided.
Each of us had a weapon...I, a pistol tucked in my belt.

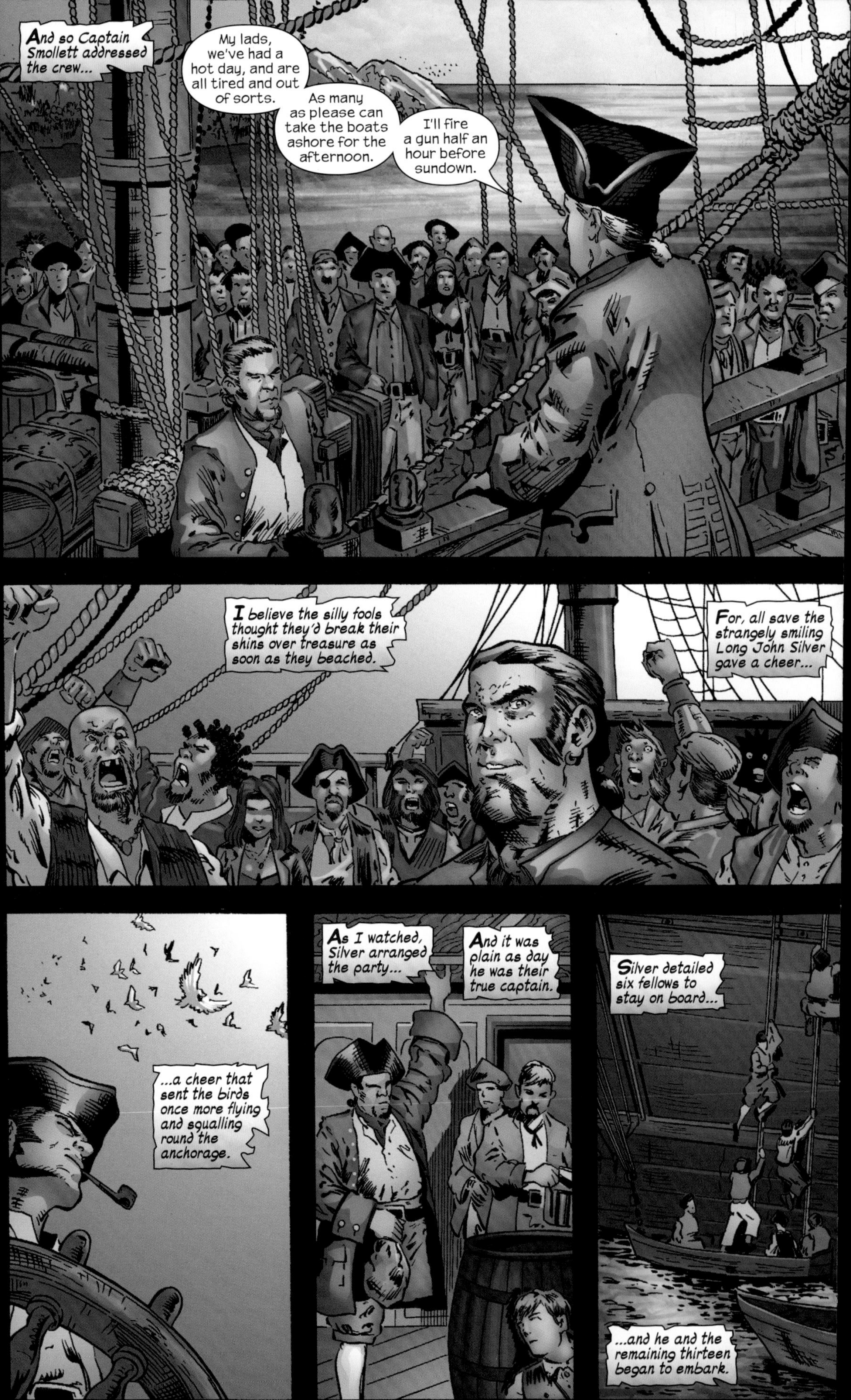
And so Captain Smollett addressed the crew...
My lads, we've had a hot day, and are all tired and out of sorts.
As many as please can take the boats ashore for the afternoon.
I'll fire a gun half an hour before sundown.
I believe the silly fools thought they'd break their shins over treasure as soon as they beached.
For, all save the strangely smiling Long John Silver gave a cheer...
...a cheer that sent the birds once more flying and squalling round the anchorage.
As I watched, Silver arranged the party...
And it was plain as day he was their true captain.
Silver detailed six fellows to stay on board...
...and he and the remaining thirteen began to embark.

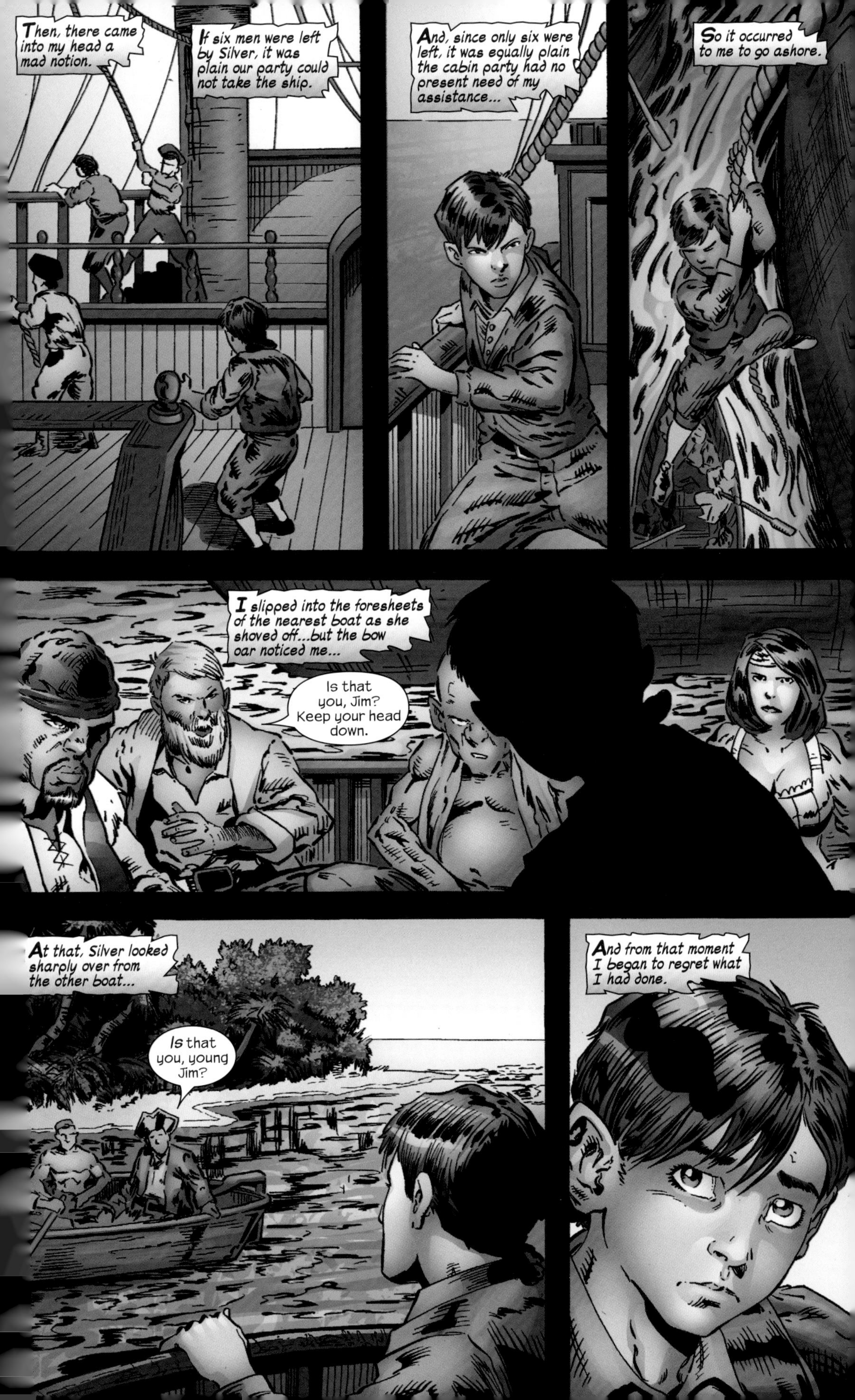

Then, there came into my head a mad notion.
If six men were left by Silver, it was plain our party could not take the ship.
And, since only six were left, it was equally plain the cabin party had no present need of my assistance...
So it occurred to me to go ashore.
I slipped into the foresheets of the nearest boat as she shoved off...but the bow oar noticed me...
Is that you, Jim? Keep your head down.
At that, Silver looked sharply over from the other boat...
Is that you, young Jim?
And from that moment I began to regret what I had done.

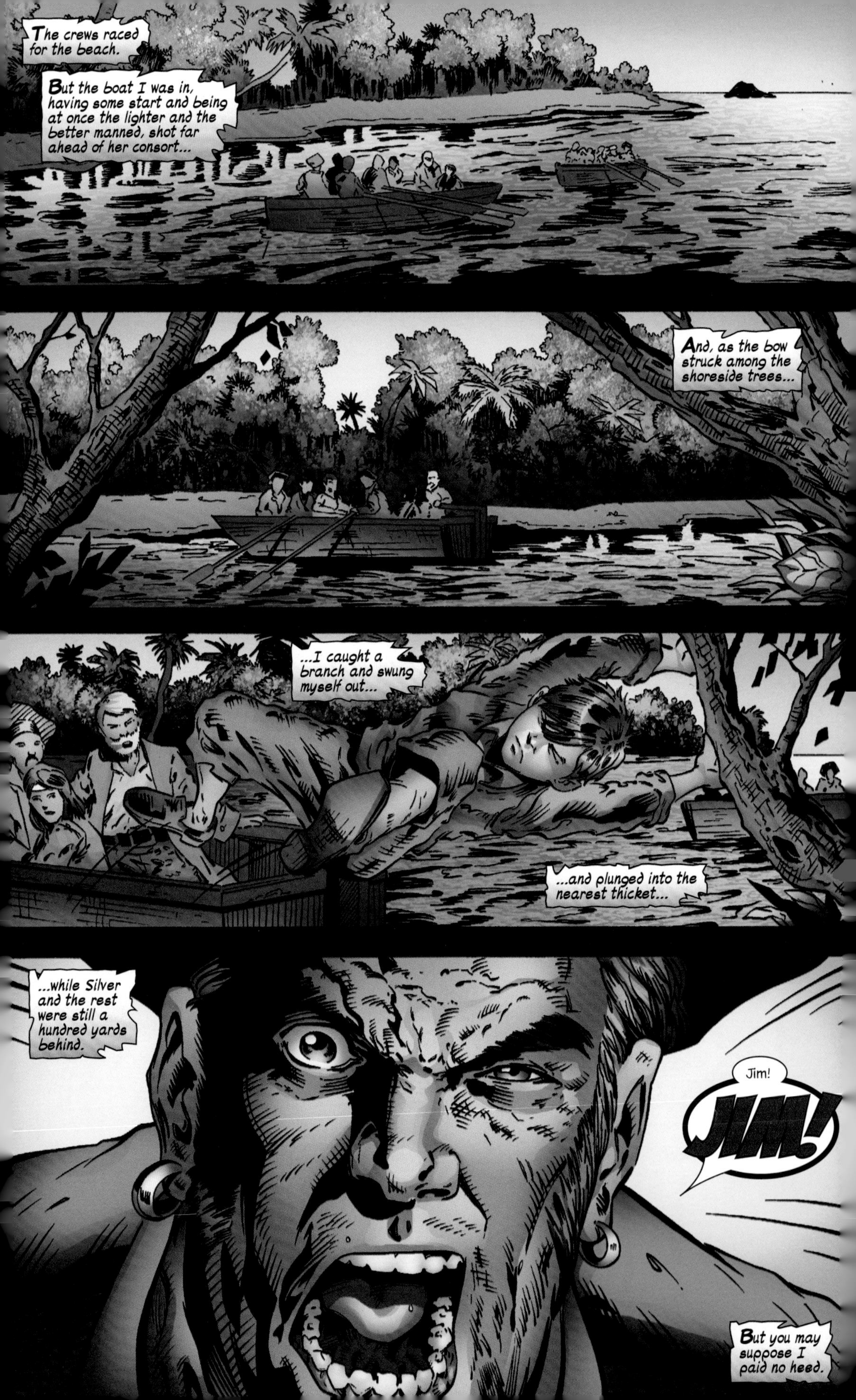
The crews raced for the beach.
But the boat I was in, having some start and being at once the lighter and the better manned, shot far ahead of her consort...
And, as the bow struck among the shoreside trees...
...I caught a branch and swung myself out...
...and plunged into the nearest thicket...
...while Silver and the rest were still a hundred yards behind.
Jim!
JIM!
But you may suppose I paid no heed.

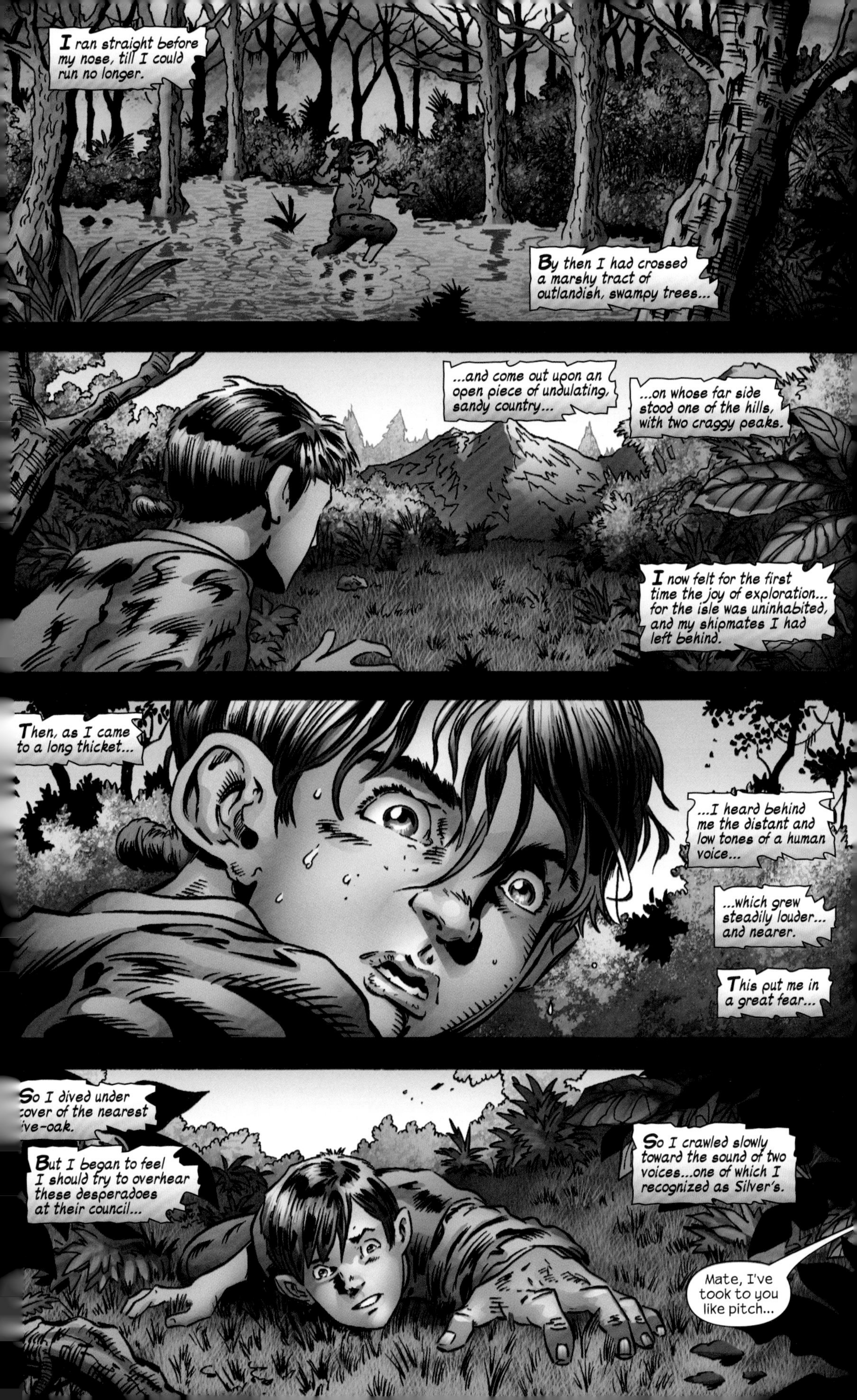
I ran straight before my nose, till I could run no longer.
By then I had crossed a marshy tract of outlandish, swampy trees...
...and come out upon an open piece of undulating, sandy country...
...on whose far side stood one of the hills, with two craggy peaks.
I now felt for the first time the joy of exploration... for the isle was uninhabited, and my shipmates I had left behind.
Then, as I came to a long thicket...
...I heard behind me the distant and low tones of a human voice...
...which grew steadily louder... and nearer.
This put me in a great fear...
So I dived under cover of the nearest ive-oak.
But I began to feel I should try to overhear these desperadoes at their council...
So I crawled slowly toward the sound of two voices...one of which I recognized as Silver's.
Mate, I've took to you like pitch...

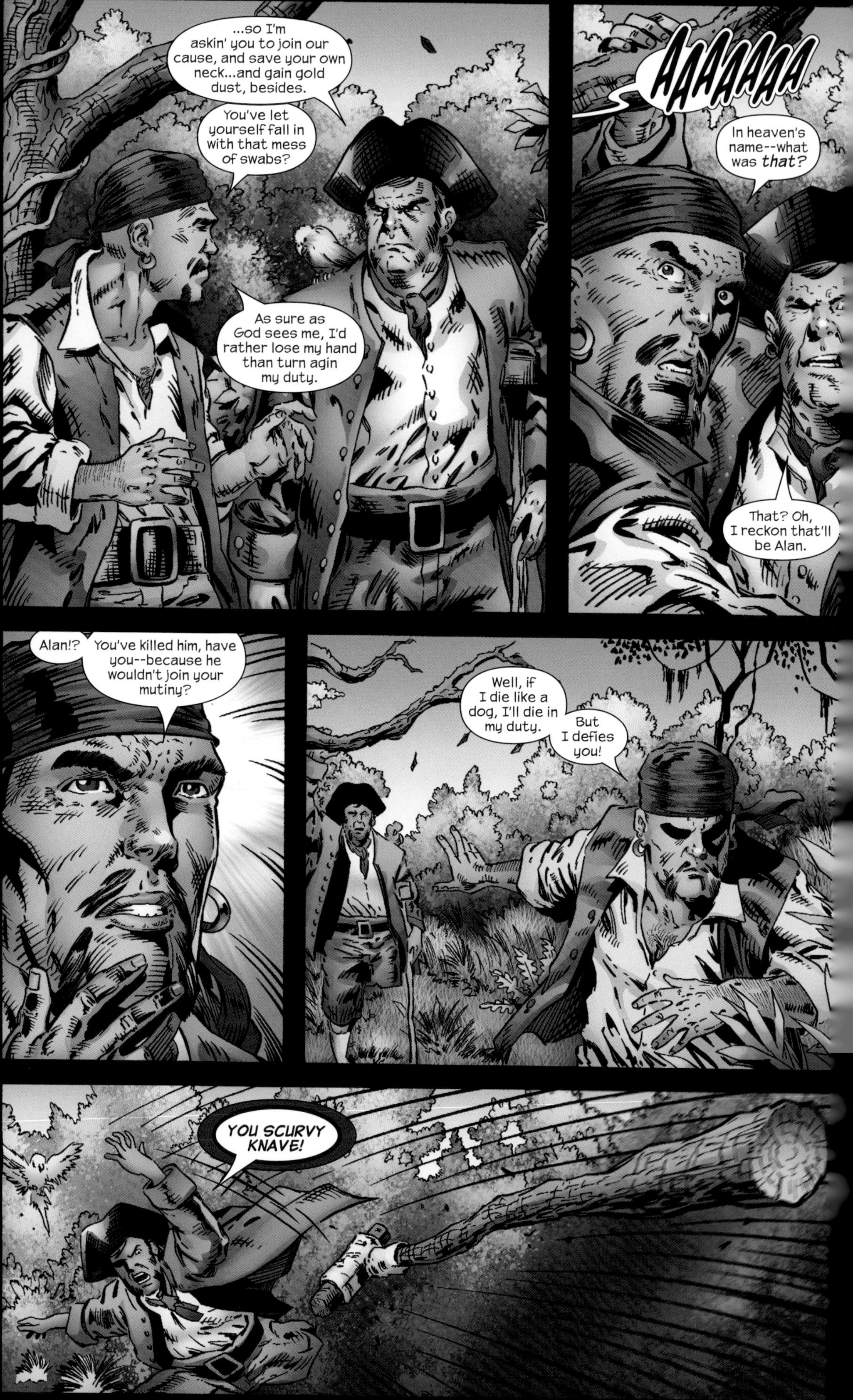
...so I'm askin' you to join our cause, and save your own neck...and gain gold dust, besides.
You've let yourself fall in with that mess of swabs?
As sure as God sees me, I'd rather lose my hand than turn agin my duty.
AAAAAAA
In heaven's name--what was *that?*
That? Oh, I reckon that'll be Alan.
Alan!?
You've killed him, have you--because he wouldn't join your mutiny?
Well, if I die like a dog, I'll die in my duty.
But I defies you!
YOU SCURVY KNAVE!

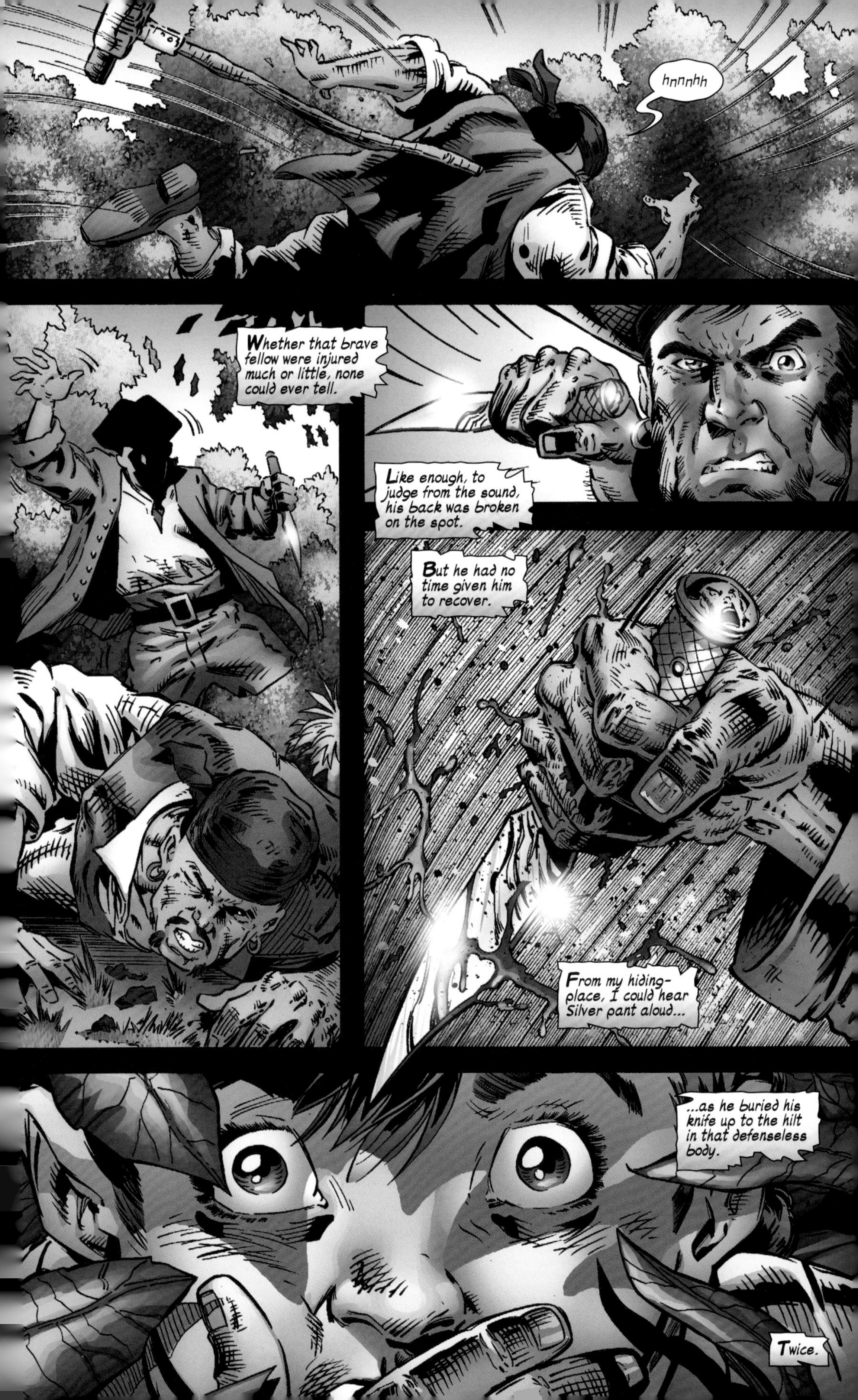
hnnnhh
Whether that brave fellow were injured much or little, none could ever tell.
Like enough, to judge from the sound, his back was broken on the spot.
But he had no time given him to recover.
From my hiding-place, I could hear Silver pant aloud...
...as he buried his knife up to the hilt in that defenseless body.
Twice.

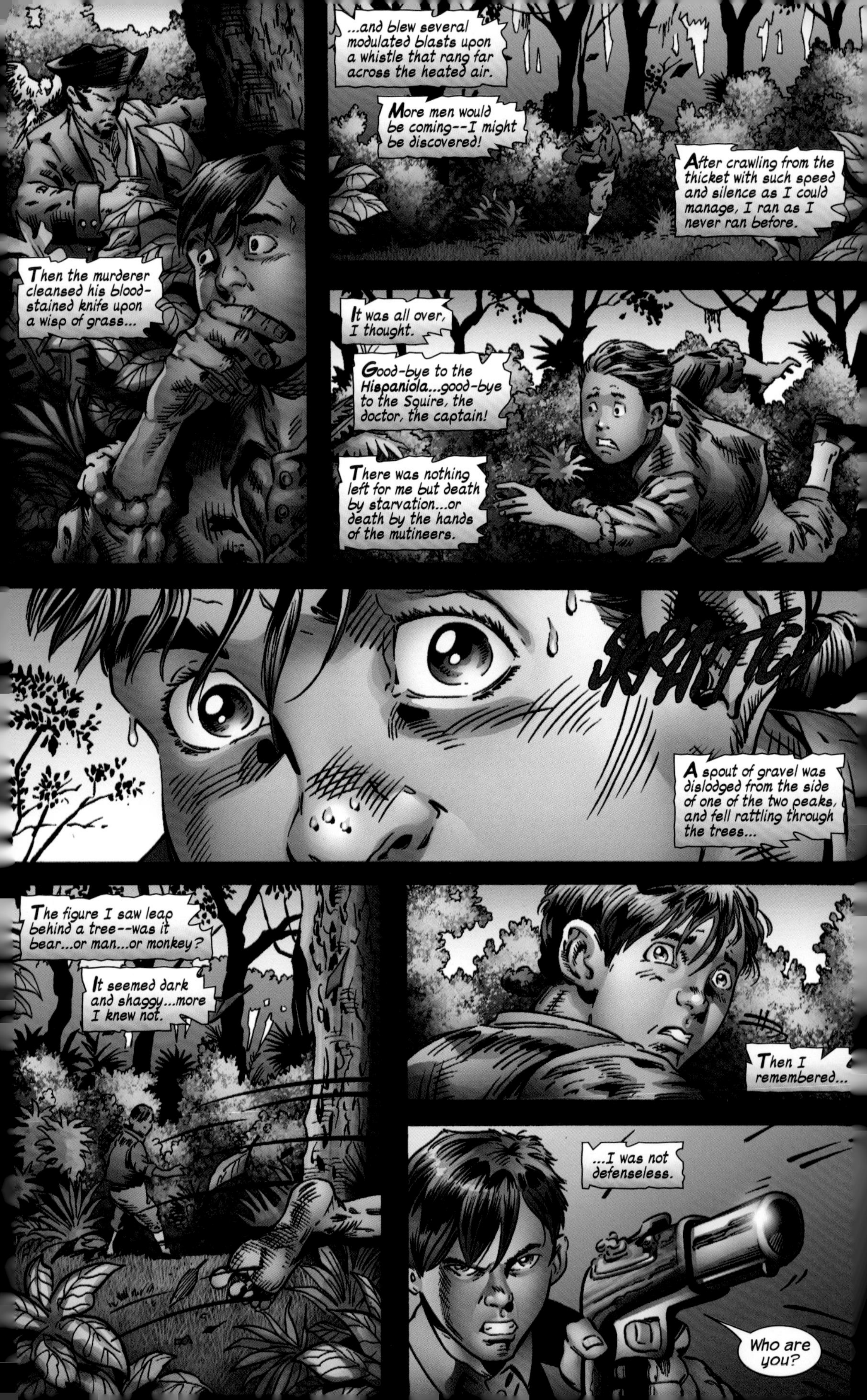
Then the murderer cleansed his blood-stained knife upon a wisp of grass...
...and blew several modulated blasts upon a whistle that rang far across the heated air.
More men would be coming--I might be discovered!
After crawling from the thicket with such speed and silence as I could manage, I ran as I never ran before.
It was all over, I thought.
Good-bye to the Hispaniola...good-bye to the Squire, the doctor, the captain!
There was nothing left for me but death by starvation...or death by the hands of the mutineers.
SKRATCH
A spout of gravel was dislodged from the side of one of the two peaks, and fell rattling through the trees...
The figure I saw leap behind a tree--was it bear...or man...or monkey?
It seemed dark and shaggy...more I knew not.
Then I remembered...
...I was not defenseless.
Who are you?

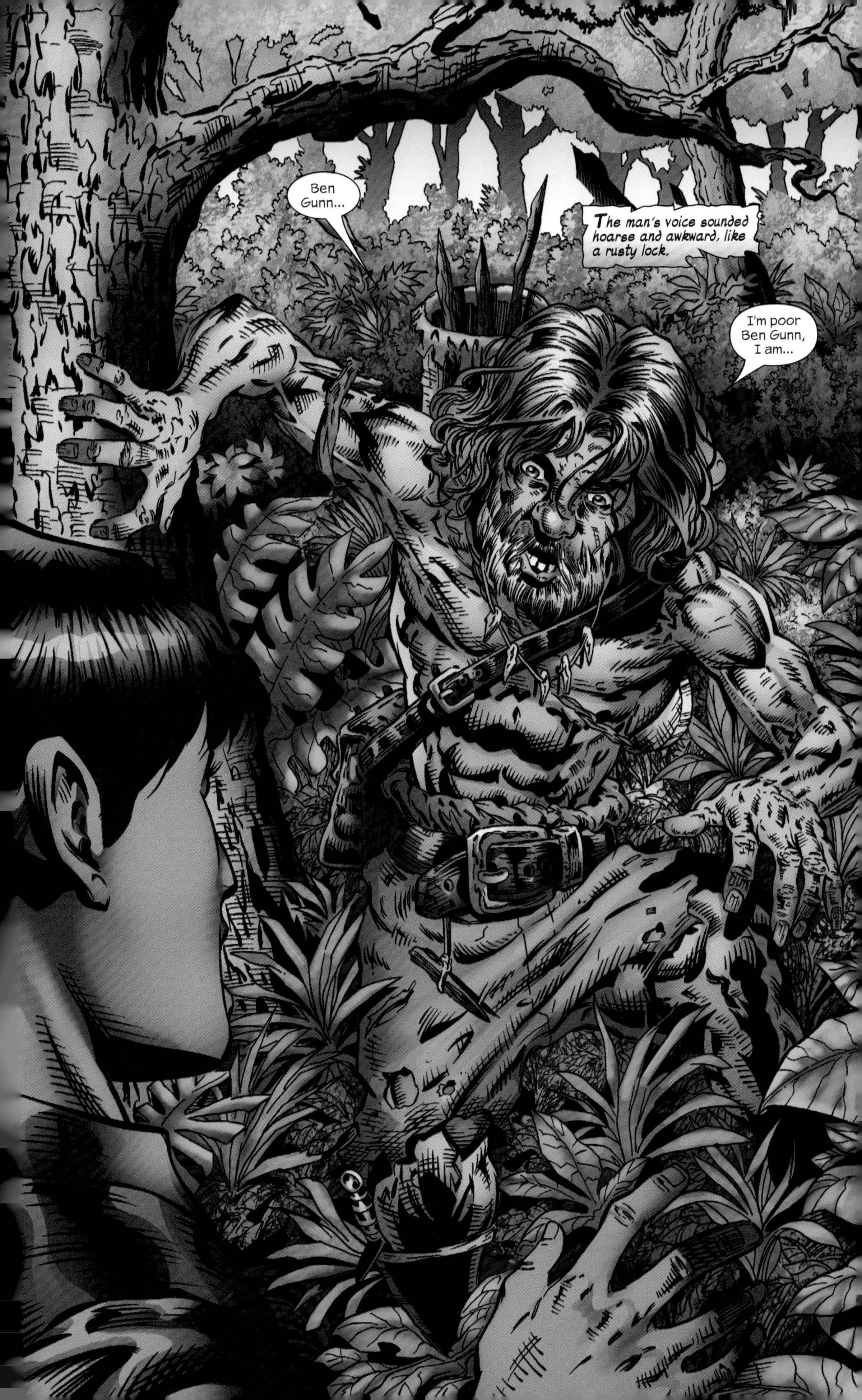
Ben Gunn...
The man's voice sounded hoarse and awkward, like a rusty lock.
I'm poor Ben Gunn, I am...

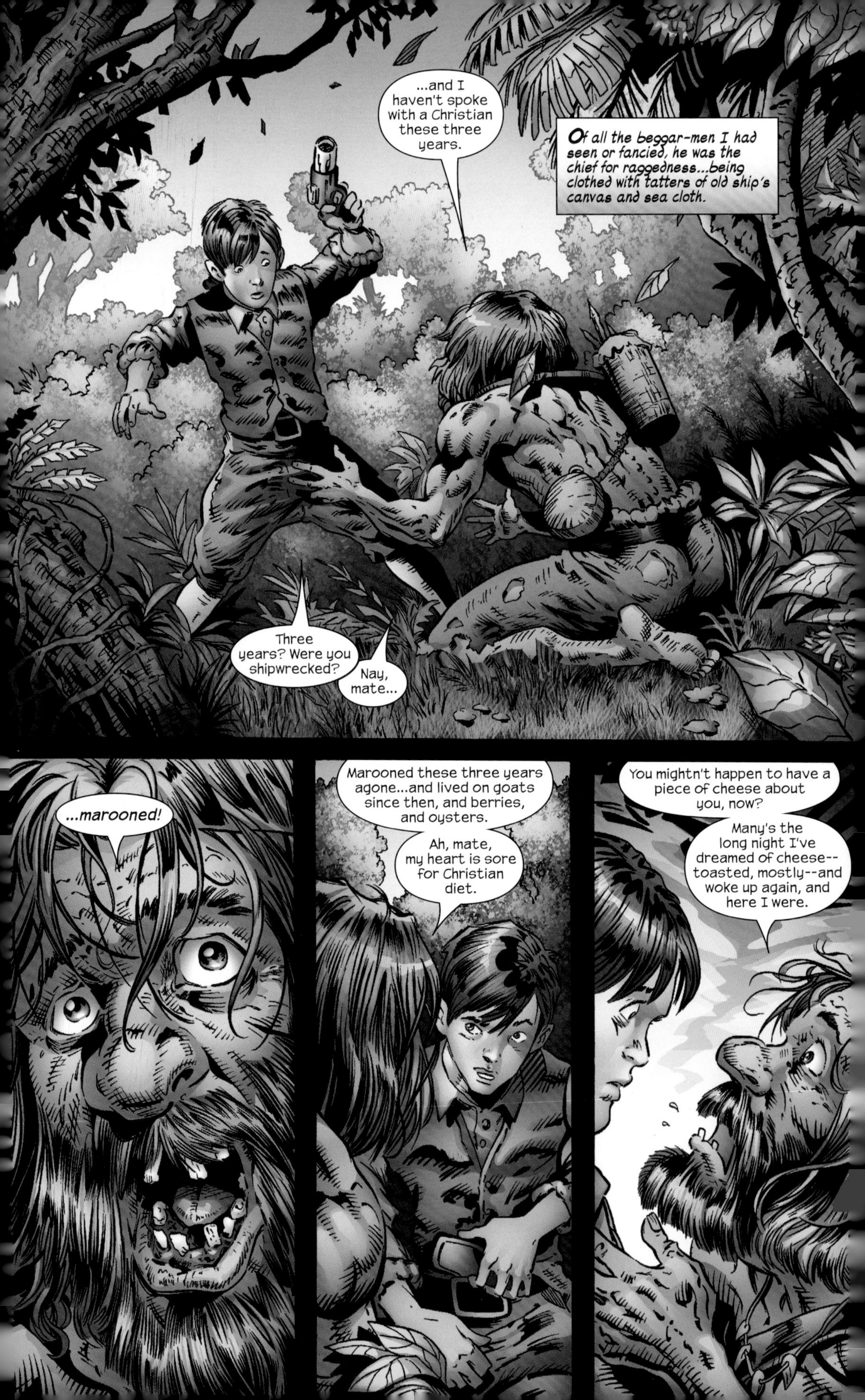
...and I haven't spoke with a Christian these three years.
Of all the beggar-men I had seen or fancied, he was the chief for raggedness...being clothed with tatters of old ship's canvas and sea cloth.
Three years? Were you shipwrecked?
Nay, mate...
...marooned!
Marooned these three years agone...and lived on goats since then, and berries, and oysters.
Ah, mate, my heart is sore for Christian diet.
You mightn't happen to have a piece of cheese about you, now?
Many's the long night I've dreamed of cheese--toasted, mostly--and woke up again, and here I were.

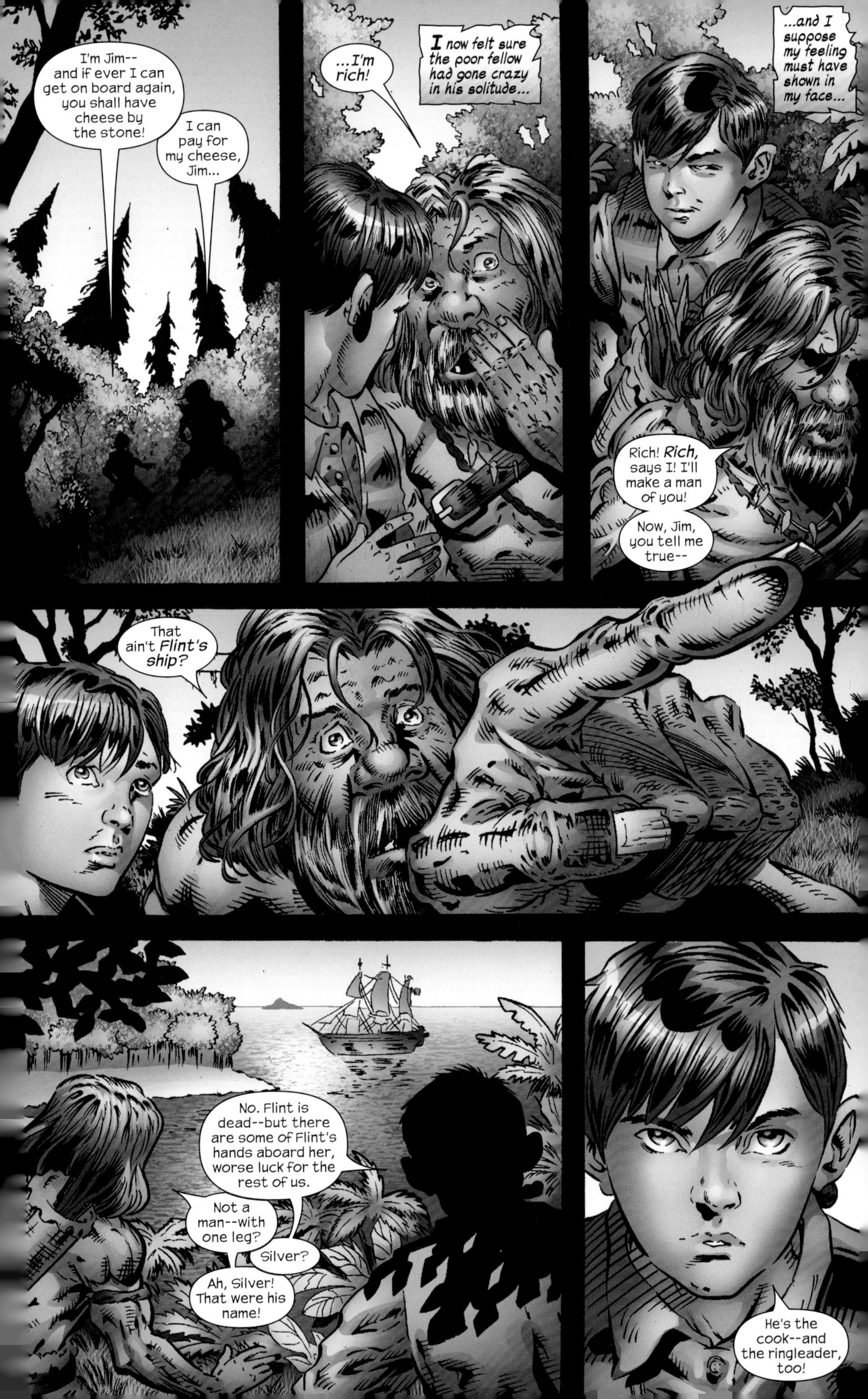
I'm Jim-- and if ever I can get on board again, you shall have cheese by the stone!
I can pay for my cheese, Jim...
...I'm rich!
I now felt sure the poor fellow had gone crazy in his solitude...
...and I suppose my feeling must have shown in my face...
Rich! Rich, says I! I'll make a man of you!
Now, Jim, you tell me true--
That ain't Flint's ship?
No. Flint is dead--but there are some of Flint's hands aboard her, worse luck for the rest of us.
Not a man--with one leg?
Silver?
Ah, Silver! That were his name!
He's the cook--and the ringleader, too!

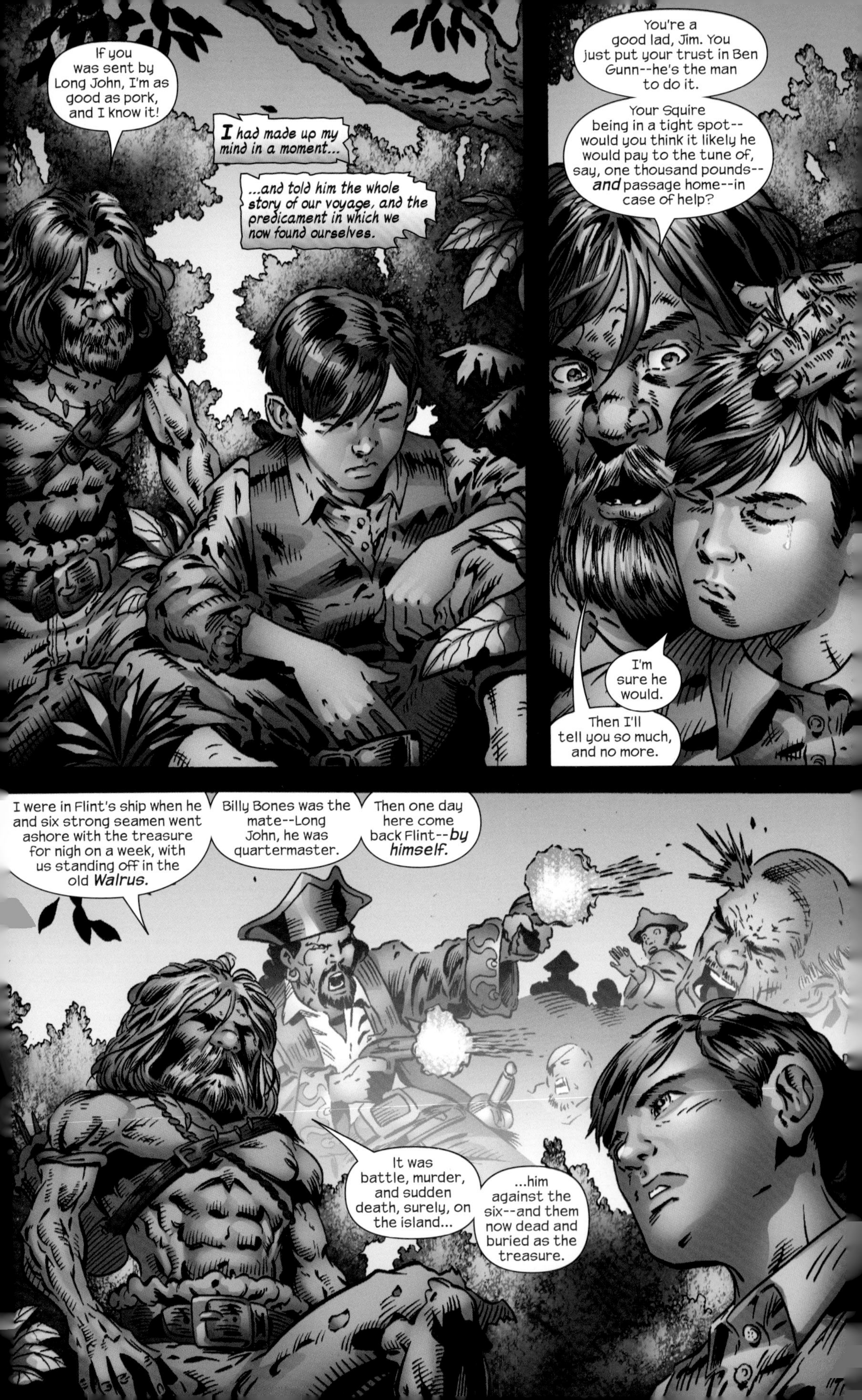

If you was sent by Long John, I'm as good as pork, and I know it!
I had made up my mind in a moment...
...and told him the whole story of our voyage, and the predicament in which we now found ourselves.
You're a good lad, Jim. You just put your trust in Ben Gunn--he's the man to do it.
Your Squire being in a tight spot--would you think it likely he would pay to the tune of, say, one thousand pounds--and passage home--in case of help?
I'm sure he would.
Then I'll tell you so much, and no more.
I were in Flint's ship when he and six strong seamen went ashore with the treasure for nigh on a week, with us standing off in the old Walrus.
Billy Bones was the mate--Long John, he was quartermaster.
Then one day here come back Flint--by himself.
It was battle, murder, and sudden death, surely, on the island...
...him against the six--and them now dead and buried as the treasure.

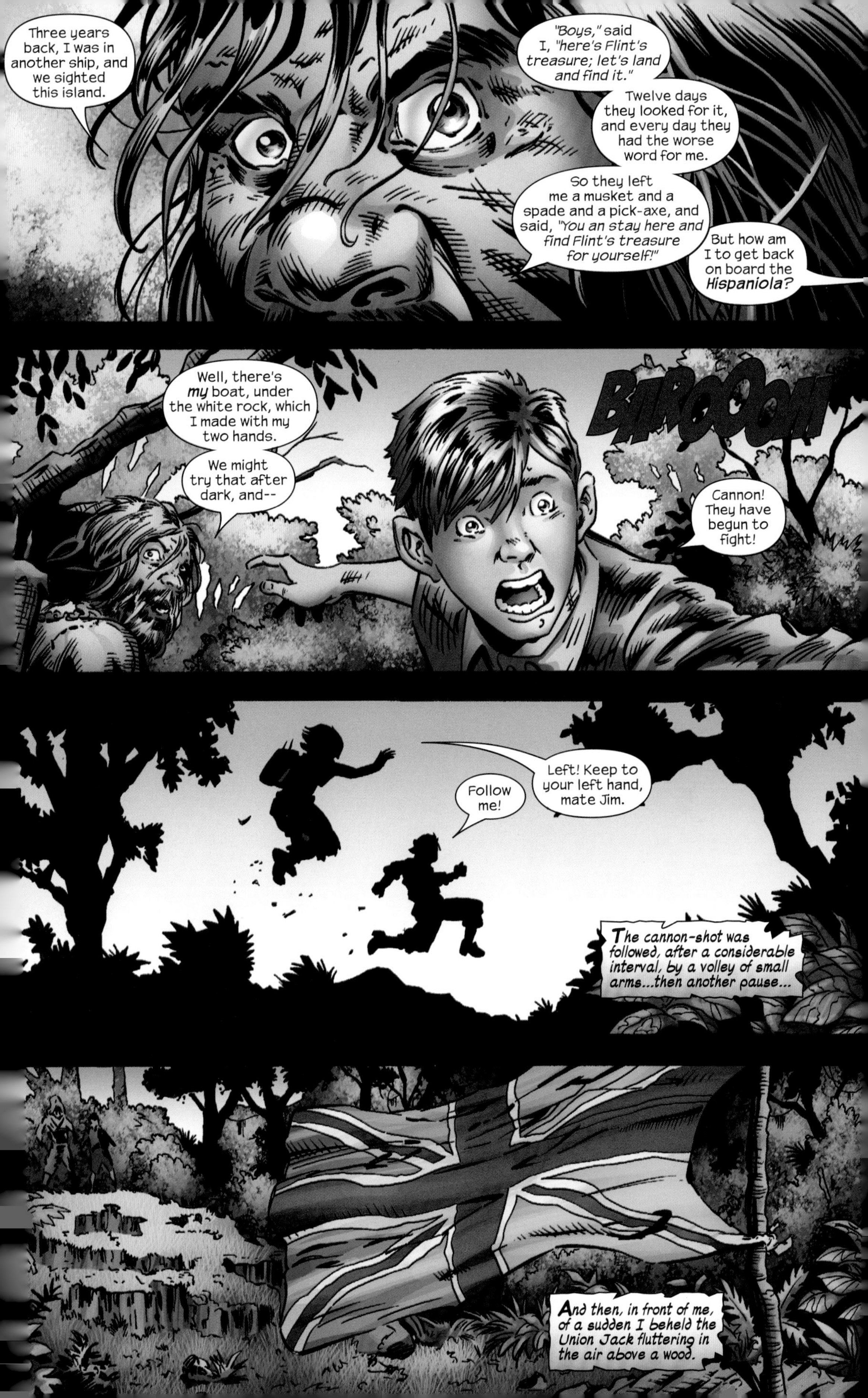

Three years back, I was in another ship, and we sighted this island.
"Boys," said I, "here's Flint's treasure; let's land and find it."
Twelve days they looked for it, and every day they had the worse word for me.
So they left me a musket and a spade and a pick-axe, and said, "You an stay here and find Flint's treasure for yourself!"
But how am I to get back on board the Hispaniola?
Well, there's my boat, under the white rock, which I made with my two hands.
We might try that after dark, and--
BAROOOM
Cannon! They have begun to fight!
Left! Keep to your left hand, mate Jim.
Follow me!
The cannon-shot was followed, after a considerable interval, by a volley of small arms...then another pause...
And then, in front of me, of a sudden I beheld the Union Jack fluttering in the air above a wood.

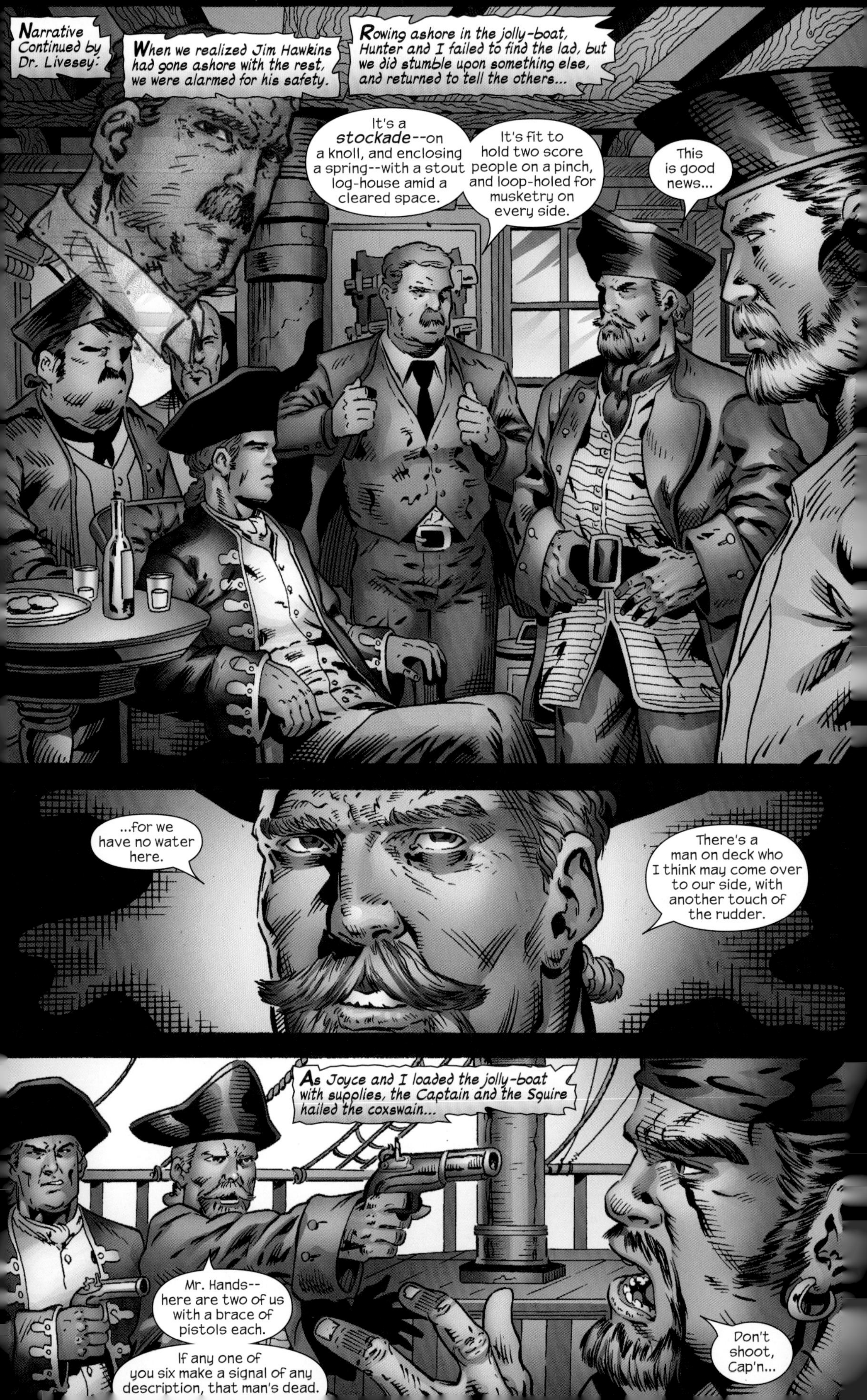
Narrative Continued by Dr. Livesey:
When we realized Jim Hawkins had gone ashore with the rest, we were alarmed for his safety.
Rowing ashore in the jolly-boat, Hunter and I failed to find the lad, but we did stumble upon something else, and returned to tell the others...
It's a stockade--on a knoll, and enclosing a spring--with a stout log-house amid a cleared space.
It's fit to hold two score people on a pinch, and loop-holed for musketry on every side.
This is good news...
...for we have no water here.
There's a man on deck who I think may come over to our side, with another touch of the rudder.
As Joyce and I loaded the jolly-boat with supplies, the Captain and the Squire hailed the coxswain...
Mr. Hands-- here are two of us with a brace of pistols each.
If any one of you six make a signal of any description, that man's dead.
Don't shoot, Cap'n...

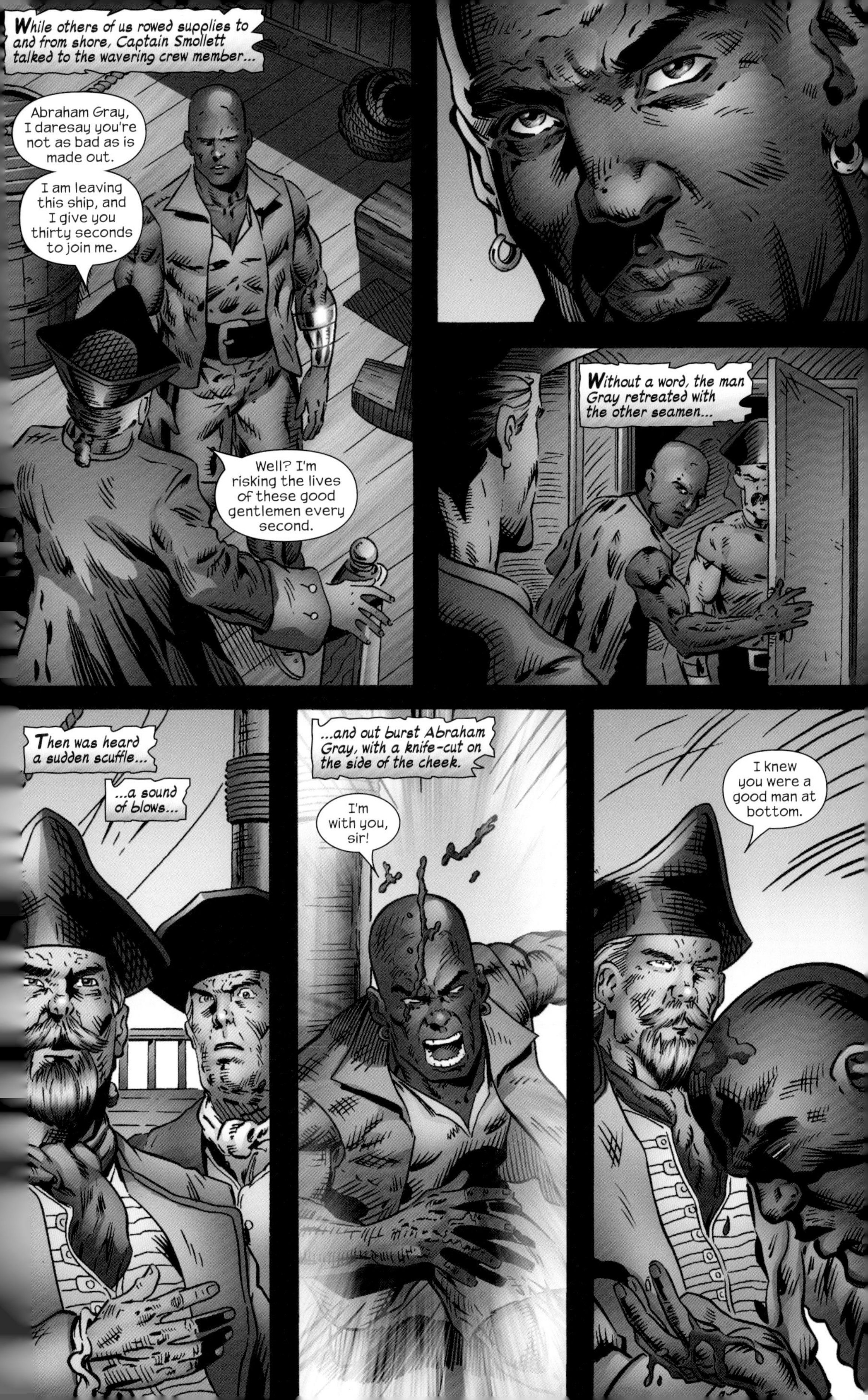
While others of us rowed supplies to and from shore, Captain Smollett talked to the wavering crew member...
Abraham Gray, I daresay you're not as bad as is made out.
I am leaving this ship, and I give you thirty seconds to join me.
Well? I'm risking the lives of these good gentlemen every second.
Without a word, the man Gray retreated with the other seamen...
Then was heard a sudden scuffle...
...a sound of blows...
...and out burst Abraham Gray, with a knife-cut on the side of the cheek.
I'm with you, sir!
I knew you were a good man at bottom.

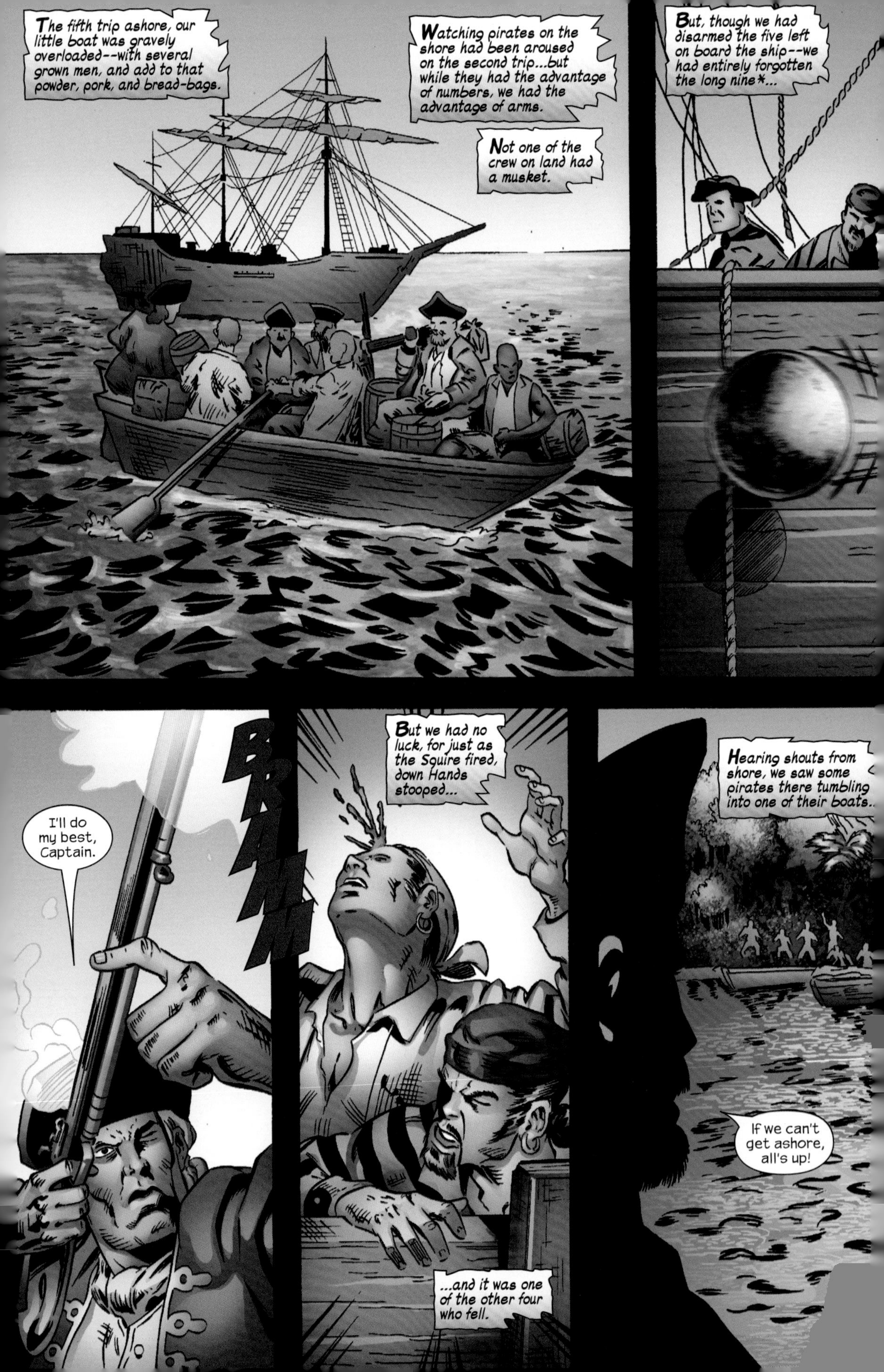

The fifth trip ashore, our little boat was gravely overloaded--with several grown men, and add to that powder, pork, and bread-bags.
Watching pirates on the shore had been aroused on the second trip...but while they had the advantage of numbers, we had the advantage of arms.
Not one of the crew on land had a musket.
But, though we had disarmed the five left on board the ship--we had entirely forgotten the long nine*...
I'll do my best, Captain.
BRAMM
But we had no luck, for just as the Squire fired, down Hands stooped...
...and it was one of the other four who fell.
Hearing shouts from shore, we saw some pirates there tumbling into one of their boats...
If we can't get ashore, all's up!

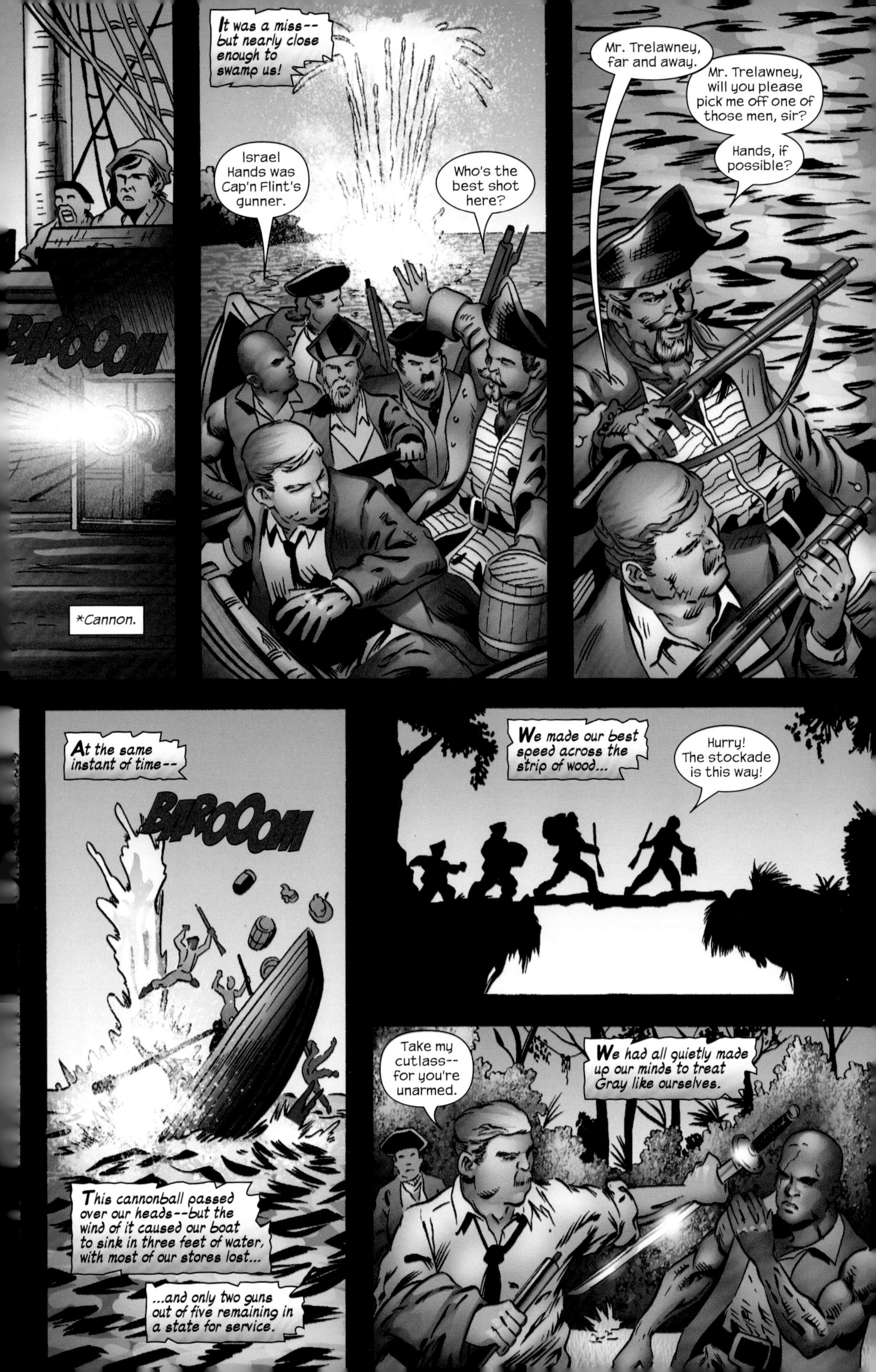
BAROOOM
*Cannon.
It was a miss--but nearly close enough to swamp us!
Israel Hands was Cap'n Flint's gunner.
Who's the best shot here?
Mr. Trelawney, far and away.
Mr. Trelawney, will you please pick me off one of those men, sir?
Hands, if possible?
At the same instant of time--
BAROOOM
This cannonball passed over our heads--but the wind of it caused our boat to sink in three feet of water, with most of our stores lost...
...and only two guns out of five remaining in a state for service.
We made our best speed across the strip of wood...
Hurry! The stockade is this way!
Take my cutlass--for you're unarmed.
We had all quietly made up our minds to treat Gray like ourselves.

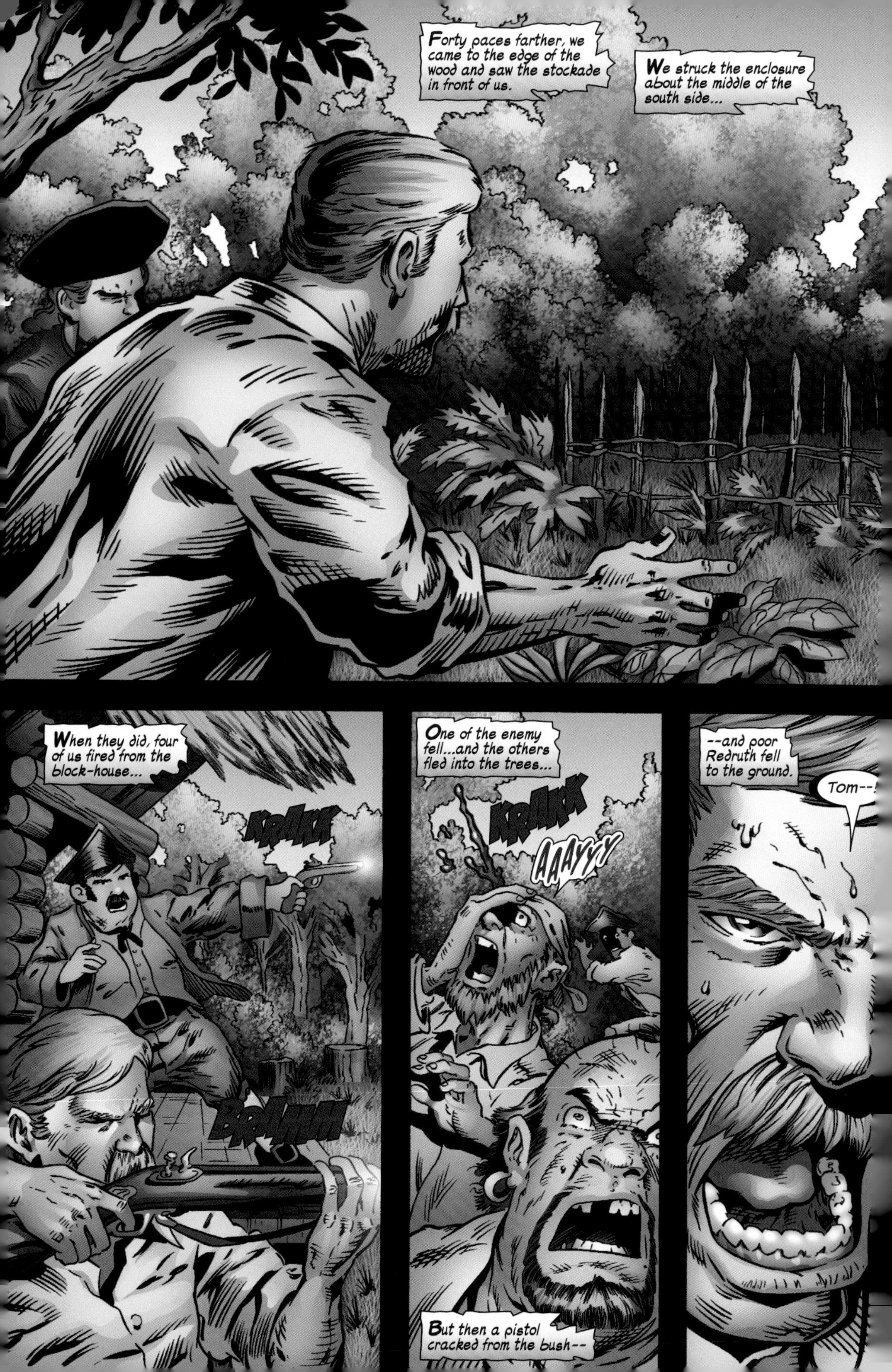

Forty paces farther, we came to the edge of the wood and saw the stockade in front of us.
We struck the enclosure about the middle of the south side...
When they did, four of us fired from the block-house...
KRAKK
BRAMM
One of the enemy fell...and the others fled into the trees...
KRAKK
AAAYYY
But then a pistol cracked from the bush--
--and poor Redruth fell to the ground.
Tom--!

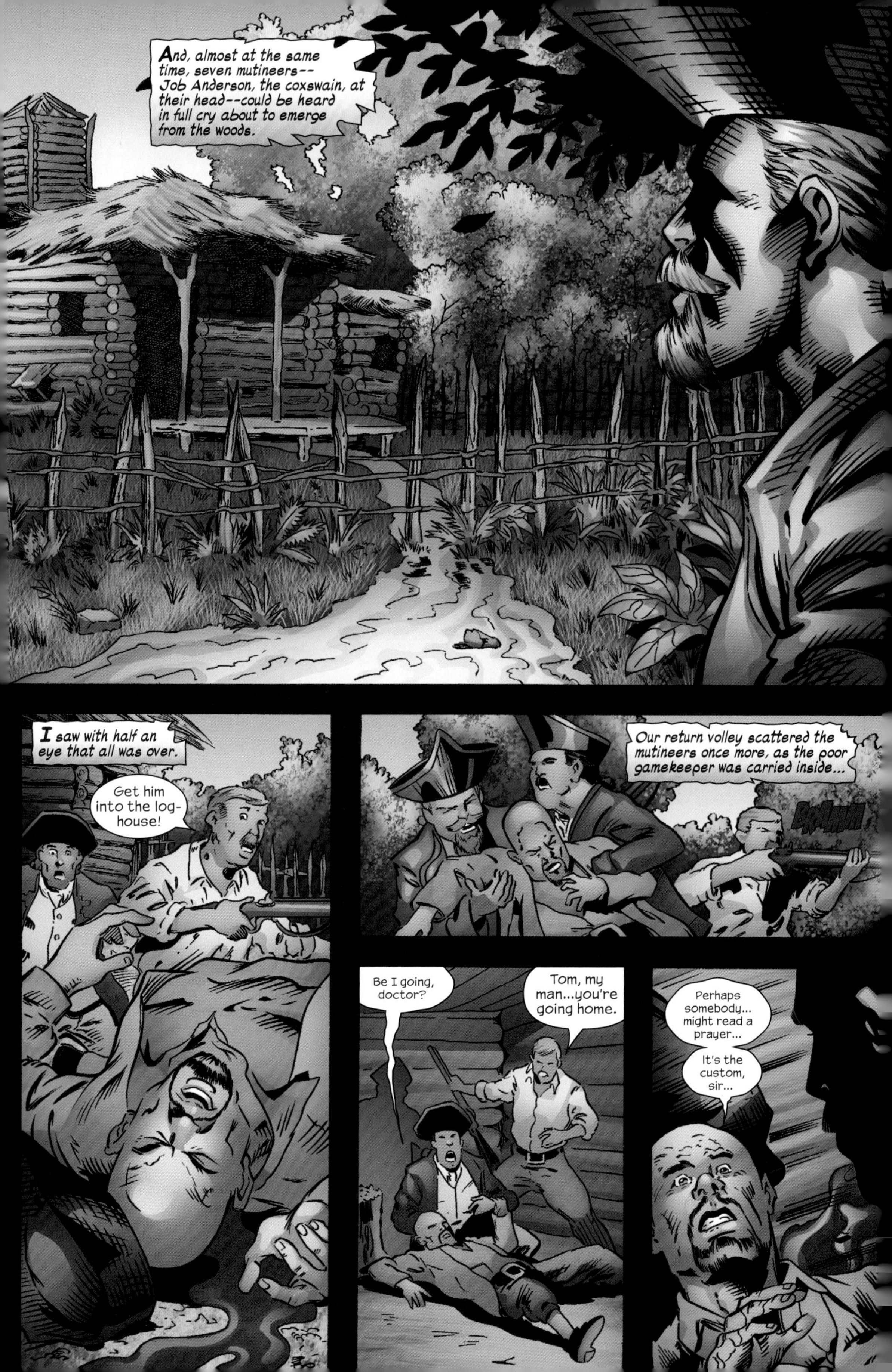
And, almost at the same time, seven mutineers--Job Anderson, the coxswain, at their head--could be heard in full cry about to emerge from the woods.
I saw with half an eye that all was over.
Get him into the log-house!
Our return volley scattered the mutineers once more, as the poor gamekeeper was carried inside...
Be I going, doctor?
Tom, my man...you're going home.
Perhaps somebody... might read a prayer...
It's the custom, sir...

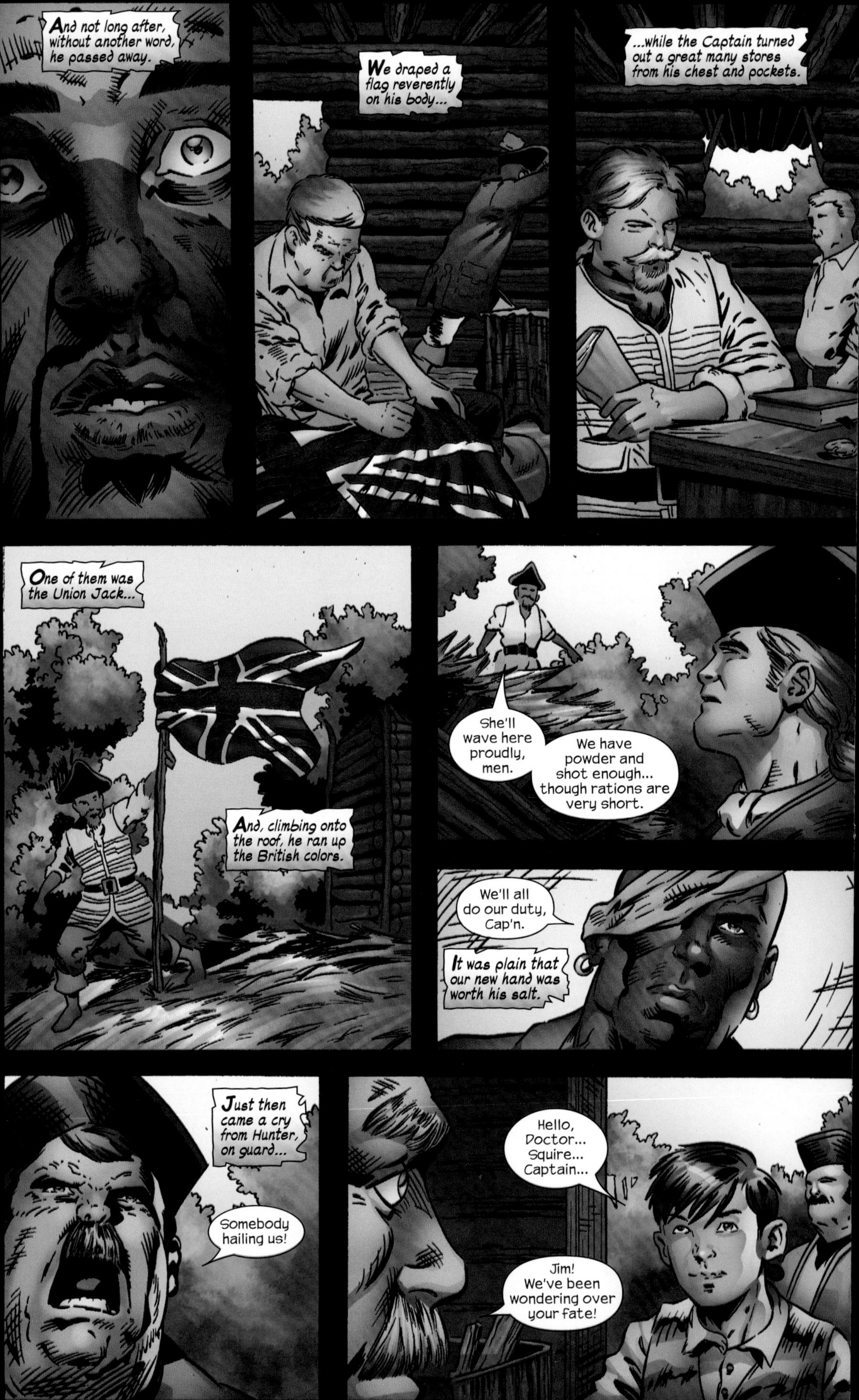
And not long after, without another word, he passed away.
We draped a flag reverently on his body...
...while the Captain turned out a great many stores from his chest and pockets.
One of them was the Union Jack...
And, climbing onto the roof, he ran up the British colors.
She'll wave here proudly, men.
We have powder and shot enough... though rations are very short.
We'll all do our duty, Cap'n.
It was plain that our new hand was worth his salt.
Just then came a cry from Hunter, on guard...
Somebody hailing us!
Hello, Doctor... Squire... Captain...
Jim! We've been wondering over your fate!

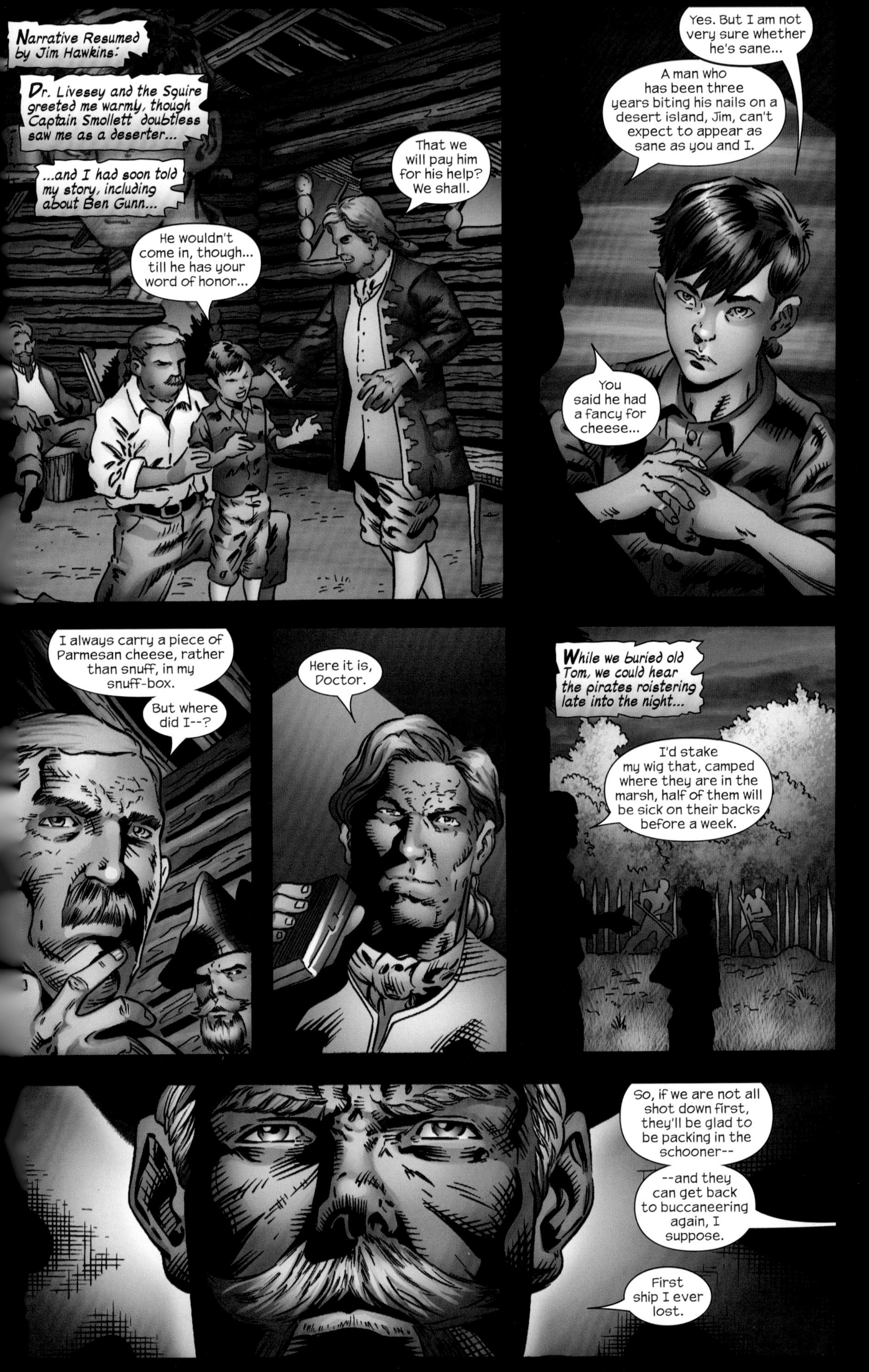
Narrative Resumed by Jim Hawkins:
Dr. Livesey and the Squire greeted me warmly, though Captain Smollett doubtless saw me as a deserter...
...and I had soon told my story, including about Ben Gunn...
He wouldn't come in, though... till he has your word of honor...
That we will pay him for his help? We shall.
Yes. But I am not very sure whether he's sane...
A man who has been three years biting his nails on a desert island, Jim, can't expect to appear as sane as you and I.
You said he had a fancy for cheese...
I always carry a piece of Parmesan cheese, rather than snuff, in my snuff-box.
But where did I--?
Here it is, Doctor.
While we buried old Tom, we could hear the pirates roistering late into the night...
I'd stake my wig that, camped where they are in the marsh, half of them will be sick on their backs before a week.
So, if we are not all shot down first, they'll be glad to be packing in the schooner--
--and they can get back to buccaneering again, I suppose.
First ship I ever lost.

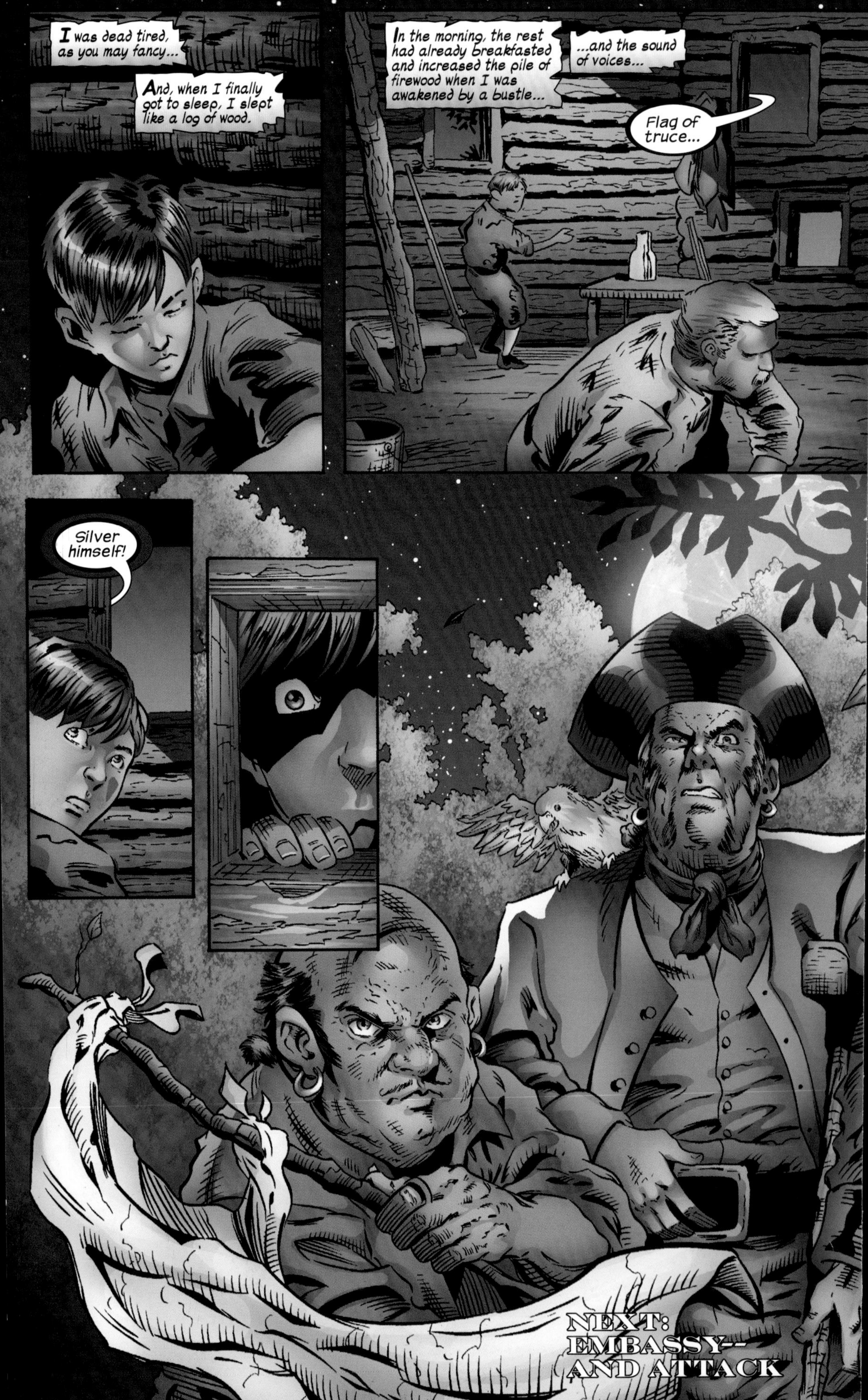
I was dead tired, as you may fancy...
And, when I finally got to sleep, I slept like a log of wood.
In the morning, the rest had already breakfasted and increased the pile of firewood when I was awakened by a bustle...
...and the sound of voices...
Flag of truce...
Silver himself!
NEXT: EMBASSY-- AND ATTACK